Erica Eggplant

Name:	Erica Eggplant
Super Power:	Super Smart
Height:	24"
Circumference:	25"
Color:	Deep purple
Location:	The Great Glass Greenhouse
Hobbies:	Reading, thinking, crossword puzzles, Sudoku, playing cello
Favorite Snack:	Baked eggplant parmesan

MISSION

Erica Eggplant will need to come up with a Super Smart plan to protect the City's gardens from Pompous Pollution's new chemical!

This book is dedicated to a future filled with smart and healthy children.

Now Available
The Super Sprowtz: Origins!
I Am Brian Broccoli and I Am Super Strong!
I Am Erica Eggplant and I Am Super Smart!

Coming Soon
I Am Colby Carrot and I Have Super Sight!
I Am Suzy Sweetpea and I Have Super Speed!
I Am Todd Tomato and I Am Super Safe!
I Am Miki Mushroom and I Am Super Soothing!
I Am Sammy Spinach and I Am Super Stretchy!
I Am Zach Zucchini and I Am a Super Swimmer!
We Are Oliver Onion and Gita Garlic and We Are Super Sweet!

THIS BOOK WAS PRINTED IN THE USA

Super Sprowtz ™, ™, A Nutrition Education Series ™,
Erica Eggplant and all related titles, logos, and characters are trademarks of Super Sprowtz LLC.

Copyright © 2010 by Super Sprowtz LLC.
Created by Radha Agrawal
Written by Radha Agrawal and Jessie Jenkins
Illustrations © 2010 by Super Sprowtz LLC.
Illustrations by Archie Valdez
Cover art by Kenny Velez and Archie Valdez
Vegetable photography by Bill Levey
All Rights Reserved.
Published in the United States of America by
Super Sprowtz LLC, P.O. Box 500, New York, NY 10014
www.supersprowtz.com
ISBN-13 978-0-9844845-3-9 ISBN-10 0-9844845-3-1
WOR 10 9 8 7 6 5 4 3 2 1

green circle
USA

ECO-FRIENDLY BOOKS
Made in the USA

The Super Sprowtz

I AM ERICA EGGPLANT AND I AM SUPER SMART!

created by Radha Agrawal

written by Radha Agrawal and Jessie Jenkins

illustrated by Archie Valdez

N

W E

S

Brian Bre...
daily work...
Spe...

Isle OF
Pollution

Rayne's f...
soccer f...

Flip flip flip.

Erica Eggplant flipped through the pages of her book. She was looking for something.

It was late afternoon one hot summer day and Erica Eggplant was in the Great Glass Greenhouse standing over a great big book.

"What could she be looking for?" Rayne wondered as she watched the super-powered eggplant flip furiously through one book and move onto the next.

Rayne was watering her vegetable garden with love, as she did every afternoon when the day began to cool.

Splish splash, splish splash went her watering can in the Great Glass Greenhouse

Erica Eggplant loved learning about new things.
She loved the smell of books and the way they
felt in her hands.

She was constantly giving Rayne a list of books to pick
up from the Public Library.

Grandpa Wyse had built Rayne a small shelf for her gardening books in the corner of the Great Glass Greenhouse.

Erica Eggplant hung a small sign above it, which read "B.O.O.K. shelf."

When Rayne asked her little eggplant friend what it meant, she replied, "Building-Our-Own-Knowledge of course!"

Of course indeed.

Rayne loved to read with Erica Eggplant in the early mornings.
In fact, the bright and colorful rooftop had become her favorite
place to curl up with a book.

Rayne was surprised to see Erica Eggplant so frazzled today. She was not only Super Smart, but she was also usually Super Organized.

But not today. Books and scribbled notes cluttered the corner of the Great Glass Greenhouse.

"What are you looking for Erica Eggplant?" asked Rayne.

"Didn't you hear the Super Sprowtz alarm go off?" Erica Eggplant replied. "Colby Carrot was scanning the City for trouble with his Super Sight and saw something brewing on the horizon. He zoomed in for a closer look and that's when he sounded the alarm!"

"What's going on?" asked Rayne.

"Pompous Pollution is about to release a new chemical from his factory!"
Erica Eggplant exclaimed.

Pompous Pollution was a tall and smoky human with a permanent
frown on his thin and pointy face. There always seemed to be a dark
gray cloud around his scary frame. He was one of the Super Sprowtz's
archenemies.

"Aha! Here it is!"
Erica Eggplant had apparently found what she was looking for.
She grabbed a pencil and began scribbling furiously.

Scribble scribble, scribble scribble.

Erica Eggplant jumped up and disappeared through the secret door at the back of Grandpa Wyse's toolshed. Rayne followed but, as usual, could only fit her head through the small door. The Super Sprowtz were already inside, awaiting Erica Eggplant's instructions.

She looked at everyone and said gravely, "Pompous Pollution is releasing a new chemical! I've analyzed the formula and when it mixes with rain, it will turn the rain into poisonous acid! Gardens all over the City will be defenseless! He's going to launch the chemical in sixty minutes!"

Erica Eggplant pulled out a giant stopwatch from her backpack. It read 0:58:20.

It was a race against time!

"I have created a recipe that will turn the acid rain back into pure water,"
Erica Eggplant continued.

"Miki Mushroom, is your cauldron ready to go?"
Miki Mushroom nodded calmly as she began to set up
her work station.

Miki Mushroom was Super Soothing and was often called upon to create healing potions in her special Super Cauldron.

Erica Eggplant started reading.

"How To Make Yummy Rain. First, each one of us must contribute some of our *Superness*. How much will depend on my careful calculations."

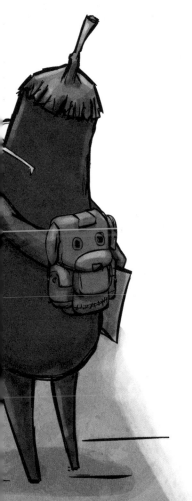

Miki Mushroom stirred her cauldron patiently as each of the Super Sprowtz stepped up and dropped in a piece of their *Superness* according to Erica Eggplant's instructions.

"Next, we'll need a map," Erica Eggplant continued. "Todd Tomato, since your Super Power is Super Safety, we need you to create a map that show the safest bike route from here to Pompous Pollution's factory!"

Todd Tomato ran over to the city map that was always on display at Headquarters and shouted, "I'm on it Erica Eggplant! We can take bike lanes the whole way!"

Erica Eggplant nodded with approval.

"Now Rayne, this is where you come in," Erica Eggplant continued.

Rayne almost bumped her head on the door frame with excitement. She had never been part of a mission before!

"Rayne, we are going to need your bicycle, your soccer ball and your soccer pump. We'll meet you downstairs at the bottom of the Super Chute in four minutes and thirty seven seconds! Any questions?" she asked, looking around the room. But there were no questions. Everyone trusted Erica Eggplant' Super Smartness. Even if they didn't fully understand her plan, they knew it would be their best chance for success.

Rayne pulled her head out of the toolshed and raced downstairs.

Swish swish swish and then...

"It's ready!" beamed the medicinal mushroom.

"Okay, Super Sprowtz, let's go!" Erica Eggplant raced out of the toolshed with her colorful team behind her. One by one, they jumped onto the Super Chute whizzed down to the street below.

Rayne was standing confidently next to her bicycle at the bottom of the chute, right on time.

She looked...different.

Swish swish swish!

Miki Mushroom was still stirring the potion.

Erica Eggplant's round glasses fogged up as
she peered over the rim of the cauldron.

"Is it ready yet? The clock is ticking!" She tapped
her foot impatiently. Miki Mushroom responded
soothingly, "Don't worry, dear, it will be ready in time."

Erica Eggplant turned to direct the rest of the
Super Sprowtz while Miki Mushroom, a twinkle
in her eye, dropped one last ingredient into her
potion, unnoticed.

Plop!

"Todd Tomato!" shouted Erica Eggplant. "Where's that map?"

Todd Tomato handed her a highlighted copy of the map.
"Using bike lanes, I've calculated that it will take us thirty-two
minutes to get through the City!"

"Uh, what are you wearing, Rayne?" asked Erica Eggplant.

"It's my Super Sprowtfit!" exclaimed Rayne proudly.
"I made it myself. What do you think?"

Her vegetable friends smiled at each other.

"We love it!" boomed Brian Broccoli. "You're *really* one of us now, *Super* Rayne!"

But this was no time for a fashion show.
Erica Eggplant checked her stopwatch and
ordered, "Onto the bike, Super Sprowtz!"

They were making good time zooming past traffic down
the empty bike lane when Colby Carrot suddenly shouted,
"Slow down! I can see a stalled school bus about a mile ahead!
It's blocking the whole street! There's no way around it!"

Erica Eggplant pulled out the stopwatch. "It's going to be close."

"Slow down Rayne!" she directed as they finally approached the factory gates. "Let's hide here," she said, pointing to an overflowing dumpster.

"So what's the plan, Erica Eggplant?" asked Zach Zucchini.

"Sammy Spinach," she yelled. "We need a ramp!"

Just before they reached the bus, Sammy Spinach launched himself off the bike and stretched his Super Stretchy self into a long, sturdy ramp.

Whoosh! The bike cruised up the leafy green ramp and easily sailed over the bus.

Rayne slowed the bike while Erica Eggplant desperately tried to think of a plan.

Then she had it.

"First, we need Rayne's soccer ball and pump," said Erica Eggplant.

Rayne emptied out her backpack. She still had no idea how a soccer ball was going to stop Pompous Pollution.

"Now, using the pump, fill the soccer ball with Miki Mushroom's potion."

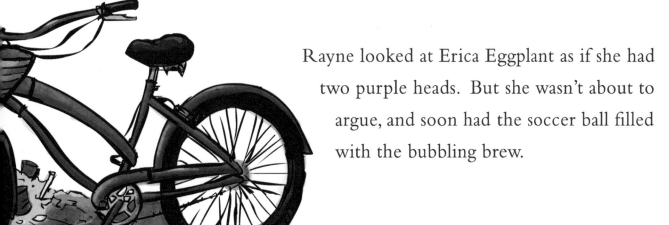

Rayne looked at Erica Eggplant as if she had two purple heads. But she wasn't about to argue, and soon had the soccer ball filled with the bubbling brew.

Erica Eggplant looked up at her solemnly.
"Rayne, you'll have one chance to kick the soccer ball into the closest smokestack. By my calculations, the acid in the pipes should melt the ball and release the potion. We've only got a few seconds left. It's up to you now!"

Rayne took a deep breath. Her friends were counting on her!

She carefully placed the soccer ball on the ground and took three steps backwards. She was the captain of her soccer team and was used to keeping her cool under pressure, but she had never been under pressure quite like this before.

THWACK!

The soccer ball flew high into the air. Everyone held their breath as they watched it soar towards the smokestack.

The only sound they heard was the ticking of the stopwatch. Five seconds to go.

Tick tick tick tick tick.

Rayne's aim was perfect! The ball disappeared into the mouth of the giant smokestack.

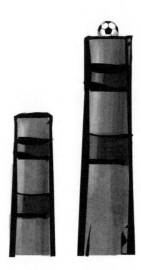

"Hooray!" the Super Sprowtz cheered.
She beamed with pride.

"Our mission isn't over yet," said Erica Eggplant.
"Time has run out. We still need to see if the
potion worked!"

A howl of rage rose from inside the factory as Pompous Pollution realized his plans were foiled again.

The City's gardens were safe, at least for now.

The Super Sprowtz climbed onto Rayne's bike and Colby Carrot led them safely home, his bright orange beam lighting their path.

The Great Glass Greenhouse sparkled in the distance. It was dinner time.

"Hooray!" Everyone cheered.

Erica Eggplant turned to Miki Mushroom, who had a satisfied look on her face. "My recipe wasn't for bubbles," said Erica Eggplant, smiling.

Miki Mushroom pointed to the parking lot where children were now jumping and laughing and replied, "But everyone loves bubbles!"

Brian Broccoli was the first to hear the rumbling.
Even his *ears* were Super Strong!

Whoosh! Rumble! Boom!

A burst of bubbles blew out of the smokestack and into the air!

The sky filled with floating bubbles.

Ten seconds went by.

The Super Sprowtz started to worry.

Another ten seconds.

Even Erica Eggplant was beginning to get nervous.

Meet Erica Eggplant, she is Super Smart!

Trying to eat more veggies? A good rule of thumb is to think in color! Purple and blue fruits and vegetables like eggplant have phytochemicals that are good for memory. Eating eggplant also helps make your child Super Smart because it contains nasunin. Nasunin is an antioxidant that helps protect brain cell membranes. Eggplant, like all plants, is cholesterol-free and may even help lower cholesterol levels!

Erica Eggplant has another great talent. She is packed full of additional antioxidants that clean out harmful free radicals in our body. This can reduce the risk of cancer.

Did you know that Erica Eggplant is a member of the nightshade family, which makes her related to Todd Tomato? Native to India, this amazing vegetable is believed to have been under cultivation for thousands of years. The french word for eggplant is *aubergine* - which is why we sometimes call Erica Eggplant the Astute Aubergine!

How do you know when Erica Eggplant is perfect for you to take home? When Erica Eggplant is ripe for the picking, she'll shine brightly for you to try and grab your attention. She will also feel firm and have no markings or mushy spots. Don't pick one that leaves an indentation in the skin after you push down. When you take her home, make sure to put her in the fridge! She likes the cool, autumn weather and your veggie drawer will make her feel at home for a few days.

For an easy and delicious way to prepare eggplant, try Chef Michel's Super Smart Egpplant Dip!

Super Smart Eggplant Dip
Chef Michel Nischan

Time: 1 hour 30 minutes   Level: Easy

  1 large purple eggplant
  1 tablespoon canola or grapeseed oil
  1 cup organic plain yogurt, well drained
  2 tablespoons local honey
  4 pieces whole wheat pita bread

Pre-heat the oven to 375°F. Pierce the eggplant at the large end with a paring knife. Rub the skin of the eggplant lightly with the oil to fully coat. Place the eggplant in oven and roast 45 minutes to an hour, or until the eggplant collapses and begins to flatten. Remove the eggplant from the oven and allow to cool to room temperature. Turn the oven down to 250°F to make the chips.

Cut the eggplant open. Use a large spoon to separate the insides of the eggplant from the skin. Discard the skin and place the insides of the eggplant into a food processor. Add the drained yogurt and honey, then blend until smooth. Add salt to taste.

Cut the pita bread into triangles and place on a cookie tray in a single layer. Bake about 25 to 35 minutes or until the chips are dry and crisp. Serve warm with eggplant dip.

View how-to video and post your favorite cooking pictures at supersprowtz.com!

As a leader in the sustainable food movement and chef with over 30 years of experience working with local producers and farmers, two-time James Beard Foundation award winner Michel Nischan wears many hats. Nischan is the owner/founder of Dressing Room: A Homegrown Restaurant, located in Westport, CT, as well as President/CEO of Wholesome Wave Foundation. The nonprofit organization's mission is to overhaul the nation's food system by increasing access to healthy, fresh and affordable locally grown food. Nischan serves on the boards of the Amazon Conservation Team, the James Beard Foundation and Harvard's Center for Health and the Global Environment. He lives in Fairfield, Connecticut with his wife, Lori and their five children.

BROCCOLI - SUPER STRONG

A Super Food! Full of nutrients, antioxidants and vitamins including A, K, and immune system-boosting vitamin C. Also contains calcium, which is important for strong bones and phytonutrients which may have anti-cancer effects.

CARROTS - SUPER SIGHT

Rich in beta-carotene, which the body converts to vitamin A. Vitamin A promotes good vision – especially at night!

EGGPLANT - SUPER SMART

Purple and blue vegetables and fruits like eggplant have phytochemicals that are good for memory. Eggplant also contains nasunin, which protects brain cell membranes. Eggplant is rich in antioxidants that can reduce the risk of cancer.

PEAS - SUPER SPEED

Contain lots of vitamins and minerals, as well as dietary fiber and protein. Green peas are a great source of energy!

ONION AND GARLIC - SUPER SWEET

Both contain sulfides, which may lower blood lipids and blood pressure and help protect against heart disease.

ZUCCHINI - SUPER SWIMMER

Full of water, zucchini also contains folate and other B vitamins, which have numerous health benefits, including lowering bad cholesterol and improving lipid profiles.

SPINACH - SUPER STRETCHY

Packed with nutrients, spinach is a rich source of vitamins A and K and many antioxidants, as well as minerals such as calcium, magnesium, manganese and iron.

TOMATO - SUPER SAFE

Technically a fruit, tomatoes contain significant amounts of vitamin C and lycopene, which have antioxidant and cancer-preventing properties.

MUSHROOMS - SUPER SOOTHING

These members of the fungi kingdom provide a significant amount of potassium, a mineral that helps the body maintain normal heart rhythm, fluid balance and muscle function.

Please note, never let your child eat mushrooms they find in the wild! Only experts can distinguish edible mushrooms from poisonous ones.

For more information, visit supersprowtz.com!

RADHA AGRAWAL

Radha is the creator of Super Sprowtz. She passionately believes that the current conversation with children about food isn't working. After opening Slice, an organic pizzeria, with her twin sister, Radha became a regular visitor to New York City public schools where she spoke about nutrition and healthy living. Alarmed by what she saw as a growing obesity epidemic among urban children, she became deeply committed to changing the way children eat. This, combined with her years of experience in story-telling as a commercial and film producer led her to create the Super Sprowtz. It is her belief that through entertaining story lines, catchy music, and lovable characters, children can see vegetables and nutrition differently. She earned her Bachelor of Science degree from Cornell University where she also played Varsity soccer. She currently lives, paints, bikes and eats locally (likely at Slice) in New York City.

JESSIE JENKINS

Jessie brings her love for healthy eating, her belief in sustainable food systems and her commitment to education to Super Sprowtz. Born and raised in New York City, Jessie taught ninth-grade science in Manhattan's Washington Heights, a neighborhood where 95% of the students qualify for the city's free-lunch program and 21% of adults are obese. While teaching, she created and fully funded the Learning Garden project - a rooftop classroom where teachers integrated gardening into their curricula. Jessie holds a BA in Environmental Studies from Oberlin College and a Masters in Science Education from Teachers College Columbia University. She lives and gardens in Brooklyn, New York.

ARCHIE P. VALDEZ

Archie P. Valdez has created art for video games, books, graphic novels, animations and commercials. Originally from the Philippines, Archie was raised in Nigeria before moving to the U.S. He studied art in San Francisco at the Academy of Art University, where he earned his Bachelor of Fine Arts with a focus in animation and illustration. Archie was initially a music and chemistry major and is still passionate about those fields - you can hear him singing sometimes when he works. Archie likes to travel, cook (in moderation), play video games and various sports, and drink coffee while sketching. He also loves to watch cartoons. Archie lives in New York City. He loves finding delicious snacks to munch on at the Farmer's Market in Union Square.

For more information
visit us at
supersprowtz.com